The Hare and the Tortoise

Retold by Susanna Davidson

Illustrated by John Joven

Reading consultant: Alison Kelly

It's spring.
Lambs are skipping.
Birds are singing.

Hedgehogs are waking up
from their winter sleep and...

sniff,
sniff,
sniffing!

As for Hare...

He leaps and bounds across
the fields and back again.

ZOOM!   ZOOM!   ZZZOOM!

"I'm so fast," says Hare.
"I'm faster than the wind!"

"I'm faster than the river!"

"I can run all day
and into the night..."

ZOOM! ZOOM! zzzZOOM!

"I can even touch the moon."

"I'm faster than you, Owl!" he shouts.

"I'm faster than you, old Mr. Badger!" he boasts.

Hare bounds up to Tortoise and laughs. "And I'm easily faster than you!"

"Humph," says Tortoise,
in a grump.

14

"Hare!" Tortoise calls out.
"I challenge you to a race!"

Owl looks
at Tortoise.

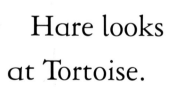

Badger looks
at Tortoise.

Hare looks
at Tortoise.

They all laugh.

"Um… Tortoise… Are you sure?" asks Badger.

"Very sure," says Tortoise.

"But you're so
s-l-o-w," whispers Owl.

"I know," says Tortoise.
"But I'm still sure."

Early the next morning,
Hare and Tortoise meet
at the starting line.

"We'll race from here to the oak tree and back," says Hare.

"One..."
hoots Owl.

"Two...

Three..."

He waves his green flag...

"GO!"

Hare leaps over the stream.

Tortoise takes another slow, small step.

By the time Hare reaches
the oak tree, he is bored.

"This is TOO easy," he
says. "I think I'll have a nap."

He lies down and shuts
his eyes.

Hare sleeps for a long time.
He sleeps as Tortoise splashes
through the stream.

He snores as
Tortoise plods up
to the oak tree...

Zzzzzzz

...and plods away again.

When Hare finally
opens his eyes, the sun
is setting in the sky.

"Oh no!" cries Hare. "The race! The race!"

He can hear the animals
cheering for Tortoise.
He leaps to his feet.

Hare flies to the finish line.

Come on, Hare!

He is faster than the river,
faster than the wind.

He leaps and bounds
across the fields...

...but he is too late.

Plod, plod, plod. Tortoise is creeping over the finish line.

"B-b-but... I'm the fastest," stammers Hare.

"He just did,"
hoots Owl.

Tortoise gives a slow, satisfied smile. He plods up to Hare.

"You see, my friend,"
he says, "slow and steady
wins the race."

About the story

The Hare and the Tortoise is one of Aesop's Fables.
These are a collection of stories first told in Greece
around 4,000 years ago. The stories always have
a message or lesson at the end. The message of
this story is 'slow and steady wins the race.'

Designed by Laura Nelson Norris
Series designer: Russell Punter
Series editor: Lesley Sims

First published in 2019 by Usborne Publishing Ltd.,
Usborne House, 83-85 Saffron Hill, London EC1N 8RT, England.
www.usborne.com Copyright © 2019 Usborne Publishing Ltd.

USBORNE FIRST READING
Level Four

Little Red Riding Hood

Retold by Rob Lloyd Jones
Illustrated by Lorena Alvarez

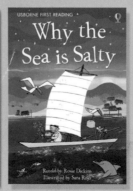

Why the Sea is Salty

Retold by Rosie Dickins
Illustrated by Sara Rojo

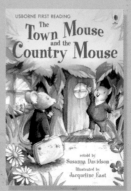

The Town Mouse and the Country Mouse

retold by Susanna Davidson
Illustrated by Jacqueline East

The Emperor and the Nightingale

based on the story by Hans Christian Andersen
Illustrated by Graham Philpot

The Inch Prince

Retold by Russell Punter
Illustrated by Matt Ward

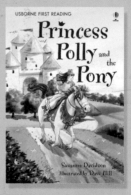

Princess Polly and the Pony

Susanna Davidson
Illustrated by Dave Hill

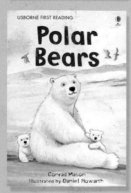

Polar Bears

Conrad Mason
Illustrated by Daniel Howarth

Butterflies

Kate Davies
Illustrated by Jana Costa

Baba Yaga The Flying Witch

Susanna Davidson
Illustrated by Sara Rojo